THE CHURCH MOUSE

Graham Oakley

ALADDIN BOOKS
Macmillan Publishing Company
New York

Aladdin Books
Macmillan Publishing Company
866 Third Avenue, New York, NY 10022

First Aladdin paperback edition 1980
New Aladdin Books edition 1987

Printed in Hong Kong

*A hardcover edition of The Church Mouse is available from
Atheneum.*

10 9 8 7 6 5 4 3 2 1

Library of Congress Cataloging-in-Publication Data

Oakley, Graham.
The church mouse.

*Summary: A lonely mouse living in a church with
only a friendly, sleepy cat for company devises a
plan to get all the mice in town to move in with him.*
[1. Mice—Fiction]   I. Title.
[PZ7.01048Ch   1987]   [E]   87-1784
ISBN 0-689-70475-5 (pbk.)

In a busy little town, not very far away, there is a church

Arthur liked living in a church. For one thing, he was very fond of music, particularly if it was loud.

and in the church there lived a mouse whose name was Arthur.

Also, if the verger had filled the font, he could go and mess about in his boat,

or practise the crawl, if the weather was warm enough.

But he liked it best because it was safe. Sampson, the church cat, had listened to so many sermons about the meek being blessed and everybody really being brothers that he had grown quite frighteningly meek and treated Arthur just like a brother.

But sometimes Arthur got a bit depressed.

One reason for this was his diet. All he ever had to eat were sweets the boys dropped during choir practice. You might say that it wouldn't make you depressed, but you are not a mouse. It made Arthur fat and bilious and it didn't do his teeth any good either.

and when he felt like having a chat, Sampson always seemed to be having one of his little day-long naps.

Then one afternoon, when he was reading, an idea popped into his head, and . .

But worst of all, he was lonely, for in the whole of that church there was not one other mouse,

as the parson was at that very moment passing by, Arthur told him all about it. The parson rather liked the idea, at least he said he was willing to give it a try.

For a moment Arthur was quite carried away. Then,

not being a mouse to let the grass grow under his feet, he rushed out of the church and into the town to put his idea into practice.

And what an awful place the town was,
much worse than he had imagined.

He almost gave up his idea, but then he
thought, "If it's always as nasty as this,

everybody is bound to agree to my
plan." So he hurried on . . .

W. JONE

HIGH QUALITY
DAIRY PRODUCE

CHEESE

ESTAB

ENGLISH & CO

and only paused once all the rest of the way.

He went into the first likely-looking
house he came to, knocked at the mousehole,

and introduced himself to the mouse
who answered. Straight away she asked
him in to meet her husband for she
knew that anybody who lived in a church
must be a pretty decent sort of person.

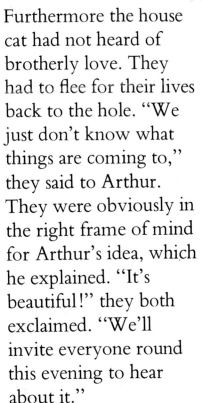

"And stop that this minute!" the mouse-mother suddenly shouted. "You could be electrocuted!"

Over tea they chatted about life and things, but Arthur could see that his new companions were a bit down in the dumps. After tea they took Arthur on a tour of the premises. "Look at that thing," they grumbled. "People leave them lying about and they can be dangerous."

Furthermore the house cat had not heard of brotherly love. They had to flee for their lives back to the hole. "We just don't know what things are coming to," they said to Arthur. They were obviously in the right frame of mind for Arthur's idea, which he explained. "It's beautiful!" they both exclaimed. "We'll invite everyone round this evening to hear about it."

So that evening, when everybody had assembled and stopped shuffling and coughing, Arthur stood up, cleared his throat, and began, without any beating about the bush.
"My idea is this. You all come and live at the church. It's warm, quiet, and I've got Sampson, the church cat, right under my thumb . . . er . . . almost. The parson says if we do a few odd jobs we'll be paid in cheese, best quality. He's expecting us tomorrow morning, if you want to come."
Everybody thought the idea simply splendid, except the schoolmouse who said something about Arthur thinking he was the Pied Piper of Hampstead or somewhere, but everybody shushed him. A vote was taken on what kinds of cheese the parson should buy, and the result was: one hundred for Cheddar, ninety-nine for Cheshire, seventy for Wensleydale, fifty for Caerphilly, forty-two for something with holes in it that no one could pronounce, thirty for walnut whirls but that was discounted because the voters were under age, and one for Afghanistan goatsmilk cheese. That was ignored because it was only the schoolmouse trying to be clever.

Next morning all the mice pinned up
forwarding addresses, and followed
Arthur to their new home.

One or two things took some getting used to, but . . .

on the whole everything went very well. The mice kept their half of the bargain and worked quite hard every day. They made sure that the flowers were always fresh and artistically arranged. They polished the congregation's shoes while they listened to the sermon. If there was a wedding they all went outside to pick up the confetti, and if anyone had thrown rice they picked that up too and made a big rice pudding for supper. After his fourth helping the schoolmouse always said he would have preferred a good risotto, but everyone just laughed.

The young ones were still sulking about the walnut whirl business, so Arthur let them tidy up after the choirboys.

As for polishing the brasses, everybody loved that because they could sneak glances at their reflections without appearing vain.

The parson kept his half of the bargain, too. Each Friday . . .

he put the different kinds of cheese in the vestry. The schoolmouse was given another chance to choose and asked for Edam, not because he liked it (he said) but because its beautiful red crust appealed to his artistic nature. Everybody just smiled, particularly when he made himself sick by eating too much of it.

Every evening after supper the grown-ups sat around the vestry stove and took turns frightening each other with horrible stories about dogs. They meant cats really, but they always said dogs so as not to hurt Sampson's feelings.

Sampson himself did baby-sitting, and *they* didn't mind a bit about hurting his feelings, or any other part of him for that matter.

But one Sunday, during the Harvest Festival service, a terrible thing happened.

Sampson, who had suffered a very bad night with the young mice, dropped off during the sermon and dreamt he was back in the days before he was reformed.

When he woke up he found he was not dreaming. He was chasing mice all over the church.

It took a bit of time to remember about brotherly love, and by that time it was too late.

IN MEMORY
OF
RICHARD TURPIN
HONEST PIOUS RIGHTEOUS
UPRIGHT LAW ABIDING
CITIZEN OF THE PARISH
WHO DEPARTED
THIS LIFE SUDDENLY
AT TYBURN
6th APRIL 1772

All the people had started to walk angrily out of the church. Nothing the parson could do would stop them. One of them said, "Either get rid of those vermin," (all the mice gasped, for no one had ever called them that before, at least not to their faces) "or we'll never come back. And what's more, they'd better not try coming back to their old holes because they'll be blocked up, and there will be a *real* cat" (here Sampson gasped) "waiting for them!"

When the church was empty, everyone turned on Sampson. "That's what comes of sleeping through the sermon," the parson said reproachfully. "I'd heard it before," mumbled Sampson, but when he saw the parson's hurt look he added quickly, "Well, something like it, anyway."
"It was all working out so nicely," the parson went on sadly, "but as it is, you'll have to go in the morning. A church is no good without a congregation, is it?"

That night the mice all sat around the vestry stove with their backs turned on Sampson and Arthur, except for the schoolmouse who pointed his finger at Sampson and said that he'd always said (though no one remembered him breathing a word of it before) that Sampson was a leopard in sheep's clothing and that a wolf couldn't change its spots and anyway, cats were all birds of a feather and so was Arthur for that matter. To his surprise everyone agreed with him for once, but only because nobody could think of anything nastier to say on the spur of the moment.

But meanwhile, something very, very fishy was going on.

Sampson's sharp ears soon let him know about it. He prowled into the transept but was back in a jiffy. "Come and look!" he hissed at Arthur.

He sounded so excited that all the other mice, who had been pretending not to listen, came out of their sulks and followed Sampson and Arthur to see what was up.

A man was taking the candlesticks off the altar. They knew he must be a terrible chap because he hadn't bothered to take his hat off in church.

The candlesticks had cost two hundred and twenty-two pounds, twenty-two and a half new pence each. The townsfolk's grandfathers had saved their farthings, their fathers had saved their ha'pennies, and they had saved their new pennies to buy them. Some people loved them so much they only came to church to make sure they were still there. "He's *stealing* them," the mice whispered to each other. But the schoolmouse said in a quaking voice that a man wasn't guilty until proved innocent and hadn't they best go back to the vestry and think about it calmly because desertion was the better part of valour.

But Arthur and Sampson knew they must do something even though they had all been sacked. Arthur stepped forward with a fairly resolute expression on his face. "Follow me, and be very, very, very, very, very," (Sampson gave him a push) "very . . . er . . . er . . .quiet," he whispered.

Fortunately the burglar
was wasting time
gloating over the
candlesticks. Everybody
tiptoed closer and . . .

Arthur tied the burglar's bootlaces together.
He had to do it himself because Sampson
could only tie granny knots.

Then Sampson obliged with his
party piece. It was supposed to be
the Song of the Nightingale but
everyone else thought it sounded
like a policeman's whistle. They
counted on the burglar thinking
so too.

He did. In his haste to escape the police (or, as Sampson insisted later, to get outside to see the nightingale), he dropped his sack, spun around, and took a great stride. Or rather, he would have if his bootlaces hadn't been tied together.

It worried them a bit when he landed on his head because they thought he might have broken some of the tiles the parson was so proud of, but it turned out there were just a few cracks. As for the burglar himself, he appeared to be sleeping like a baby.

Everybody had the idea of rolling him up in the carpet. At any rate, everybody said it was his idea afterwards. They all put their shoulders to the carpet and pushed. The schoolmouse said to the mouse beside him that he felt like a Lilliputian, but the mouse replied huffily that he couldn't stand foreign food because he was just an average English working mouse and *he* felt like a cheese and chutney sandwich, and the mouse next to him said he felt like a bread and butter pudding, and Sampson said he felt like a mouse casserole and he'd have one, too, if they didn't shut up and push.

Suddenly the burglar woke up and started shouting words that even the schoolmouse had never heard before. Then he began to struggle and the mice had to strain to stop him unrolling himself. "Do something!" they shouted at Arthur.

"Er . . . Umm . . . Ahh . . ." said Arthur decisively. Then the schoolmouse butted in. "There's only one thing to do," he said. "We must ring the bells and summon help." But by then Arthur was master of the situation. "There's only one thing to do," he cried. "We must ring the bells and summon help. Half of you follow me to the bell-tower!" And with that he dashed off like a born leader except that he went in the wrong direction and by the time he realized his mistake the others were half way there so he had to pretend he had stayed in the rear to hurry stragglers along.

When he caught up he found everybody
staring in dismay at the bell-ropes
which were tied up, well out of reach.
"Now what?" they all cried.
"Er . . . Umm . . . Ahh . . ." said
Arthur without hesitation. The
schoolmouse butted in again, saying
that Sampson could climb on the back
of a chair and reach one of the ropes,
but Sampson hadn't forgotten the
nasty names the schoolmouse had
called him in the vestry. "Wolves in
spotted sheep's feathers aren't very good
at climbing on the backs of chairs," he
mumbled sarcastically.
However Arthur had sized up the
situation. "Sampson," he said briskly,
"will climb on the back of the chair and
reach one of the ropes."
But it was no good.
Then a mouse who had lived in the
local theatre made a shy suggestion.
"I don't know whether it can be done
without sky-blue tights with sequins
on them," he added, "but we could
try."

So they did, and it worked

and they rang the bells until they thought everyone within a radius of ten miles must be awake.

The townsfolk tumbled out of bed shouting things like "Earthquake!" "Martians!" "Flood!" "Plague!" "Escaped rhinoceros!" "Anarchists!" "Apaches!" "Fire!" "The end of the world!" "Locusts!" "Vikings!" "Burst pipe!" "Students!" "Mad hedgehog!" "Icebergs!" but soon everybody was racing towards the church.

When they saw how near they had come to losing their beautiful candlesticks, the townsfolk got very peevish with the burglar. They seemed to think that he had got himself rolled up in the carpet through trying to steal that, too, but Arthur soon told them how he . . . er . . . well . . . to stretch a point, he and his friends and Sampson had trapped the burglar.

And after that, of course, there was no more talk of their having to leave the church. The parson pointed out that the mice had earned their keep for at least fifty years by saving the candlesticks, and, because of that, he said they needn't bother doing any more chores. But all the mice, or, to be honest, a few of them anyhow, said they would prefer to keep on working since it is best to keep the mind occupied. The schoolmouse let it be known that he was quite prepared to take the more advanced Sunday School classes in Philosophy, Horticulture and Train-spotting, but everybody just sighed.

As for Sampson, you might think he was very sorry about his lapse, but you would be wrong because he wasn't. The mice had been taking him a bit for granted of late, he thought, and the fact that they were frivolous giddy creatures was no excuse. They'd learnt he was not to be trifled with, and after that, whenever they needed reminding, he would just yawn and say he hoped he wouldn't drop off during the sermon, and then there would be no more giggling and tittering over silly jokes about "dogs" for at least two days.